THIS BOOK BELONGS TO:

Alexis Hollander

The Day I Could Fly

BY *Lynn Crosbie Loux*

ILLUSTRATED BY *Guy Porfirio*

NorthWord Press
Chanhassen, Minnesota

The illustrations were created using acrylic paint and colored pencil on Strathmore paper
The text and display type were set in Albertina and Banshee
Composed in the United States of America
Designed by Lois A. Rainwater
Edited by Aimee Jackson

Text © 2003 by Lynn Crosbie Loux
Illustrations © 2003 by Guy Porfirio

Books for Young Readers
NorthWord Press
18705 Lake Drive East
Chanhassen, MN 55317
www.northwordpress.com

Library of Congress Cataloging-in-Publication Data

Loux, Lynn C., date.
The day I could fly / by Lynn C. Loux ; illustrations by Guy Porfirio.
p. cm.
Summary: After a crow's black feather falls and touches her arm, a young girl becomes a crow,
viewing her world from the sky until it is time for supper.
ISBN 1-55971-866-8
[1. Flight—Fiction. 2. Crows—Fiction.] I. Porfirio, Guy, ill. II. Title.

PZ7.L95475Day 2003
[E]—dc21
2002043102

Printed in Singapore
1 3 5 7 9 10 8 6 4 2

For Joel and Catherine,

my own flown birds.

—L. C. L.

To David, devourer of books,

builder of all things

K'NEX and an

incredibly wonderful

young man.

—G. P.

I have often walked in fields
    among the trees,
and the birds who sing there
are quiet as I pass.
But once,
from the top of a tree
a crow sent down a feather.
The feather
touched my arm as it fell,
and its touch of black
and dancing colors
turned my arms into wings.

I was lifted on the winds
and circled over my house and yard.
I could see my brother and sister.
I could see my grandfather working
in our garden far below.
"Grandpapa, Grandpapa, look at me!"
I called to him in my crow's voice.
But he did not seem to notice
his crow girl
with black wings that danced
in the sunlight.

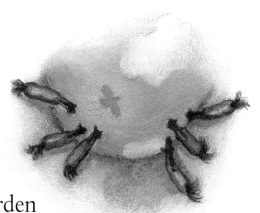

Beyond the garden
I could see our neighbor's horses
drinking silently from the pond.
From the sky
they looked like the little toy horses
I keep in a toy chest in my room.
I flew down to our neighbor's pasture
and watched the horses
grow bigger and bigger and bigger,
as I landed beside them.

When I was a real girl
I could come to the fence
and bring the horses
carrots from our garden.
While they nibbled them,
their whiskery chins
would tickle my hand,
and I could pet their soft noses.
But a crow girl is so small
she has to be careful in a forest
made of legs and tails
of horses.

In the pond
I could see my reflection.
I cocked my head left,
then right
to look at my sleek, feathered face,
and I smiled, a crow smile.
I noticed there were minnows
that seemed as big as trout
darting along the edge of the pond,
and I waded out to them,
testing the water
with small crow feet.

A sudden wind crinkled the water
and I flew up into the air,
even higher than before.

Far below me,
I could see the town where I live,
and the park where I like to play.
I circled over the playground
and watched friends
as they went down the slide
and played together
on the jungle gym.
Some were pushing their swings
way up into the sky.

"Look at me—I can fly!"
I called down to them.
But they did not know
their crow friend
with her sleek, black wings.

In swirls of warm air
I flew out toward the mesa.
Then, below me
a patch of bright gold
drew me down from the sky.
I landed beside a row
of huge sunflowers,
their golden heads and brown faces
hanging heavy with seeds.
My heart danced, a crow dance,
as I picked up fallen seeds
with my new beak.

I flew to a cottonwood
and asked if I might make a nest
in its wide branches.
It said it would be happy
to hold my home
made of twigs and mud
and bits of string
and tiny black feathers
from my crow body.

When it was finished
I sat in my nest
with my wings peacefully gathered,
and I was content.

I woke from a cozy nap
to see that the small, white clouds
of afternoon
had grown big and dark
over the mesa.
Suddenly,
there was a zigzag of light,
and thunder crashed around me.
The smell of rain grew closer and closer,
and my feathers ruffled
in the strong breeze.

Then, from far away
I heard my mother's voice
calling me home for supper.

Quickly, I flew home
and landed on the windowsill.
I looked into our house
and saw my brother and sister
as they played together.
My father sat quietly talking
with Grandfather
at the kitchen table.
Behind me,
I could feel,
I could hear the storm
hurrying down from the mesa.
I wanted to be inside
with my family.

I flew from the window
out to the garden
where my mother stood
calling me.
As I flew,
a feather dropped
from my beautiful wing.
The feather was soft and black
and had colors dancing on it.
As it floated
and gently touched the ground,
I became a real girl
again.

I ran to my mother,
saying, "Here I am, here I am!"
in my girl's voice.
I was happy
to be with my family again,
and we laughed together
as we set the table for supper.
Outside we could hear
deep rumbles of thunder,
and soon rain began falling
against the windows
of our house.

After supper
my grandfather asked me
where I had been today.
I told him
that I had walked in the fields
among the trees,
and that from the top of a tree
a crow had sent down a feather.
I told him the feather
had given me real wings.
"But Grandpapa," I said,
"when the storm came
I didn't want to be alone,
even though I could fly
and make my own nest."

He smiled,
a grandfather smile.
From his pocket
he took a beautiful feather
that was soft and black
and had colors dancing on it.
"I think this must belong to you,"
he said, gathering me into his arms
and handing me the feather.
"Someday," he said, "you will know
when it is the right time
for you to fly."

LYNN CROSBIE LOUX is a published poet who teaches with California Poets in the Schools, a statewide artist-in-residence program. She shares with students her own love of language and helps them find their own amazing poetic voices.

Lynn was inspired to write *The Day I Could Fly* when she saw a crow's feather fall from the top of a tree. She lives in the Eastern Sierra with her husband, David.

GUY PORFIRIO is frequently accused of having his head in the clouds, and we think this book proves it. Flying around the house with his family, he occasionally takes time out to sketch and paint.

Guy has illustrated numerous books for children, including *Clear Moon, Snow Soon*, a book about Christmas written by Tony Johnston, and *Papa's Gift*, an inspirational story written by Kathleen Long Bostrom. Guy lives in Tucson, Arizona, with his wife and their two children.